Trade-or-Treat Halloween

For everyone who loves a treat,
especially kids with food allergies,
who always choose the safest sweet!

LIBRARY OF CONGRESS CONTROL NUMBER: 2009903028
ISBN 978-0-9822150-2-9

PP parent perks inc.

P.O. Box 95024
Newton, Massachusetts 02495
www.parentperksinc.com

Authors: Heather Mehra and Kerry McManama
Illustrations: ©Michael Kline Illustration (dogfoose.com)
Design: JoeLeeDesign.com
Printed in China

the No Biggie bunch™

Trade-or-Treat Halloween

BY
Heather Mehra & Kerry McManama

ILLUSTRATIONS BY
Michael Kline

FOR KIDS CREATIVELY COPING WITH FOOD ALLERGIES

"Wow! Check out that moon!" Natalie exclaimed.

The No Biggie Bunch looked up at the night sky. They were all excited to be trick-or-treating on Halloween.

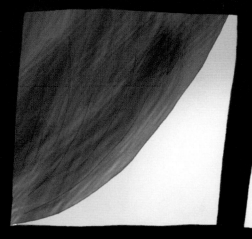

"Trick-or-treat!" chimed
the No Biggie Bunch as a
neighbor tossed candies
into their No Biggie Bags.

Greta looked into her bag. "Yippee!
I see three candies I *CAN'T* eat because
of my gluten allergy!" she shouted.

"I'm allergic to dairy," Davis said. "I think I'll make a magic spaceship too!" He would swap his candy that contained milk for tons of juicy jelly beans.

"I could send my peanut candies to outer space," Paige said. She hoped the man on the moon would send her a new princess crown.

"I know what you're thinking, Princess Paige!" Scotty joked.

"Let's keep trick-or-treating!"

"There's lots of candy I'm allergic to — lots to trade!" Davis said.

The whole No Biggie
Bunch gathered at the
door of the most festive
house on the block.
Scotty rang the
doorbell.

The No Biggie Bunch took one small step toward the door and one giant leap back as it flew open. What appeared? A bowl full of moon lollipops.

trading possibilities!

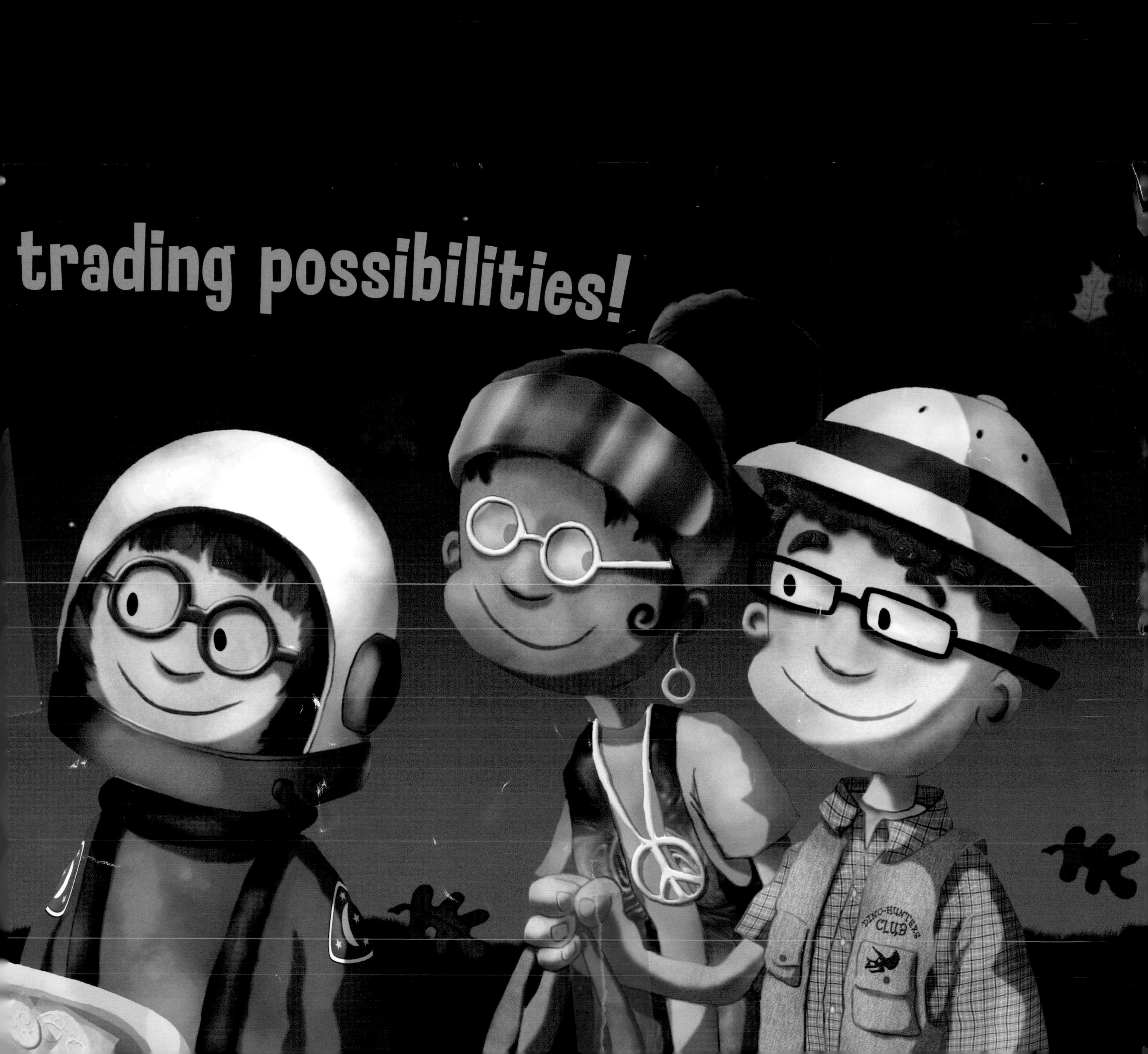

No Biggie Bag Bonus

How would you trade-or-treat
your Halloween candy?

**Glow-in-the-dark
Stickers**

Juicy Jelly Beans

**Perfect Princess
Crown**

"Remember, if Greta
eats even a tiny bit of
gluten or wheat, she
can get very sick,"
Davis reported.

"I know that," Eliot said. "But why is she so happy about it? That's a bummer!" he blurted.

"No biggie!"

Greta smiled, "I get something even cooler!"

Last Halloween, before Greta went
to bed, she put all the candy
that contained gluten into
her magic spaceship.
And then ...

Poof! In the morning, she found glow-in-the-dark star stickers — perfect for her bedroom solar system.

"Oh, I see! You did a TRADE-or-treat!"

"That's why you have such a neat outer-space room!"

"Yep," Natalie said, "And any of you can trade the candy you're allergic to for treats that are safe for you."

Greta

Greetings from outer space! I'm Greta. I'm allergic to gluten.

Scotty

Hey, sports fans! My name is Scotty. I'm allergic to Soy.

Paige

I'm Paige, the fairest princess in all the land. I'm allergic to peanuts.

Meet the No Biggie Bunch

Davis

Hello, fellow explorers. I'm Davis and I love dinosaurs. I'm allergic to dairy.

Natalie

Hi, friends. My name is Natalie and I'm artsy. I have no food allergies.

Eliot

Howdy, partners! They call me Cowboy Eliot. I'm allergic to egg.

The Mission of the No Biggie Bunch

The No Biggie Bunch is a diverse group of kids who handle the social challenges of food allergies with poise and panache.

The adventures of Davis, Natalie, Paige, Eliot, Scotty and Greta are neither technical nor medical. Their stories are meant to act as springboards for conversation among children, parents, teachers, friends and family members.

The No Biggie Bunch doesn't speak about limitations or medications. They focus on allergen-free celebrations and smart preparation.

Focus on fun and all you can do and soon you'll be saying,

"No Biggie" too!